Karen's Worst Day

Also in the Babysitters Little Sister series:

Karen's Witch

Karen's Roller Skates

Karen's Kittycat Club

Look out for:

Karen's School Picture

Karen's Little Sister

Karen's Worst Day

Ann M. Martin

Illustrations by Susan Tang

Hippo Books
Scholastic Children's Books
London

Scholastic Children's Books,
Scholastic Publications Ltd,
7-9 Pratt Street, London NW1 0AE, UK

Scholastic Inc.,
730 Broadway, New York, NY 10003, USA

Scholastic Canada Ltd,
123 Newkirk Road, Richmond Hill,
Ontario, Canada L4C 3G5

Ashton Scholastic Pty Ltd,
P O Box 579, Gosford, New South Wales,
Australia

Ashton Scholastic Ltd,
Private Bag 1, Penrose, Auckland,
New Zealand

First published in the US by Scholastic Inc., 1989
First published in the UK by Scholastic Publications Ltd, 1992

Text copyright © Ann M. Martin, 1989

ISBN 0 590 55009 8

Typeset by A.J. Latham Ltd, Dunstable, Beds
Printed by Cox & Wyman Ltd, Reading, Berks

BABYSITTERS LITTLE SISTER is a trademark of Scholastic Inc.

10 9 8 7 6 5 4 3 2

*This book is for
Read Marie Marcus,
Josh's little sister*

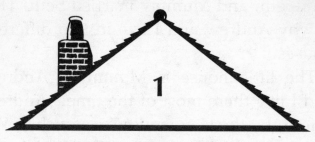

Hello, My Name Is Karen

Hi! My name is Karen Brewer and I'm six years old. I have a plastercast on my arm at the moment because I broke my wrist roller-skating two weeks ago. I had to go to hospital and it was very exciting.

Daddy and my big sister Kristy took me to hospital. That was because I was at Daddy's house for the weekend. You see, my little brother Andrew and I live sometimes with Daddy, and most of the time with Mummy.

Daddy and Mummy used to be married, but then they got divorced and then they both got married again. Daddy married Elizabeth, and Mummy married Seth. This is why Andrew and I live in two different houses.

The little house is Mummy's. Andrew and I live there most of the time. (Andrew is four, by the way, and he's very shy.) We live there with Mummy and Seth and Rocky and Midgie. Rocky is Seth's cat and Midgie is his dog. Seth likes animals and children, which is lucky for Andrew and me.

The big house is Daddy's. Andrew and I live there every other weekend, and for two weeks in the summer holidays. The big house is *really* big, and it's full of people. This is who lives at the big house besides Andrew and me: Daddy, Elizabeth, Elizabeth's children, and Shannon and Boo-Boo. Shannon is a puppy and Boo-Boo is Daddy's fat old cat. He scratches and bites and goes wild. He's really nasty.

Elizabeth has four children. They are my stepbrothers and stepsister. Charlie and Sam are really grown-up, and they go to high school. David Michael is a bit older then me; he's seven. David Michael and I fight a lot. Then there is Kristy. Kristy is one of my favourite, favourite people. She's thirteen and sometimes she babysits for Andrew and David Michael and me.

Andrew and I have two houses and two families and two of lots of other things. We each have two pairs of jeans and two pairs of trainers and two bicycles − one for the big house, one for the little house. We have books at Mummy's and books at Daddy's. We have toys at Mummy's and toys at Daddy's. This means that we don't have to take lots of things back and forth when we go from one house to the other.

I even have two stuffed cats − Moosie and Goosie. Moosie stays at the big house, and Goosie stays at the little house. For a long time I had a problem, though. My special blanket is Tickly, and there was only one Tickly. Sometimes I would forget to bring Tickly with me. Once, I was climbing into bed at Daddy's and I remembered Tickly

3

was at Mummy's so I cried. Having two houses and two families is fun sometimes, but not all the time. Anyway, finally I tore Tickly in half so now I keep half at each house.

One thing I don't have two of is roller skates. I only have one pair. But that won't matter for a long time. The doctor said I wasn't allowed to roller-skate until the plaster comes off my wrist, and that won't be for weeks.

Drat! Why did I have to fall and break my wrist anyway? I think that was the beginning of my bad luck. I have had some bad luck lately. At Mummy's house, Goosie was lost for two whole days. And I dropped my lunch tray at school and everyone laughed. And after I gave Andrew a very interesting new haircut, Mummy and Seth were angry with me.

But those were just little bits of bad luck. I didn't have a lot of bad luck until Saturday, when Andrew and I were back at the big house. I had bad luck *all* day long. It was my worst day ever. In fact, it began the night before, when I was trying to fall asleep. I just couldn't go to sleep. Even with Moosie and Tickly next to me

I tried and tried and tried. . . .

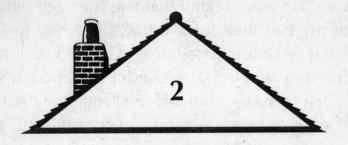

Karen's Bad Dream

"Daddy!" I called. "Daddy!"

Daddy was at my door in a flash.

"Karen, what's wrong?" he exclaimed. "Are you ill? Did you fall out of bed?"

"No," I answered. "I can't fall asleep. I can't sleep at all. I've been lying here for hours and hours."

"Darling, Kristy put you to bed twenty minutes ago," Daddy told me.

"Really?" I said. "Well, it seems like hours. Besides, I can see the witch out of my

window. And she's up to something."

I think I forgot to tell you about my witch. She lives next door. All the grown-ups say she is just an old lady who wears funny black clothes and they call her Mrs Porter. But I know better. I know she isn't *just* an old lady, and I know she has a witch's name. Her witch's name is Morbidda Destiny. Morbidda Destiny can cast spells. She has a herb garden in her back garden. That's where she grows things with strange names to use in her spells. Things like fennel and basil.

Morbidda Destiny has a black cat, as well. His name is Midnight and his eyes are round and yellow. They stare at you. Our cat Boo-Boo doesn't like Midnight, but he hates Morbidda Destiny even more. Every time he sees her, he does something odd, like run up a tree and stay there, as if his feet were glued to the trunk.

I've seen a broom next to Morbidda Destiny's front door lots of times. And she cackles like this, "Heh, heh, heh," and talks to Midnight. And once I think I saw her fly out of one of her windows on her broom. But I'm not sure about that.

"Karen," said Daddy, "how many times do I have to tell you? Mrs Porter is not a witch. She's just —"

"I know," I interrupted him. "She's just an old lady who wears funny black clothes . . .and has a broom and a black cat."

Daddy sighed. Then he pulled my curtains drawn.

"No more spying on Mrs Porter," he said.

"If you stop thinking about her, you'll fall asleep much faster."

"Okay."

"Think pleasant thoughts and you will have pleasant dreams." Daddy kissed my nose and I gave him a butterfly kiss with my eyelashes.

When he left my room, I thought very pleasant thoughts. And I did go to sleep. But I kept waking up. Each time I did, I looked at my clock. Eleven thirty, 1:28, 3:44, 5:16, 6:59. . . .

After 6:59, I was running out of pleasant thoughts. I had already thought of ice-cream and cartoons and pets and new shoes and birthdays. What was left?. . . Oh! Roller-skating.

I closed my eyes. I pictured myself in my fancy red skates, skating up and down our road.

My mind began to float away, and soon I was skating in a dream.

In the dream, I reached the end of our road and saw that I had come to a hill.

If I could just skate up that hill, I thought, then I could go zooming down the other side. The hill was very steep, but a rabbit came along and said, "I'll help you reach the top". And he did. He pushed me right up to the top.

"Thank you," I said, but the rabbit had already gone.

I peeped over the hill to see what the road looked like on the other side. There was no road — just a cliff!

Oh, well, I thought. I'll just turn around and go back the way I came. But before I could do that, I lost my balance and fell.

I was falling, falling, falling. . . .

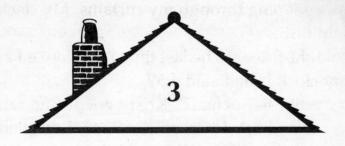

3

Kristy to the Rescue

"Aughhh!" I screamed.

I had landed on the rocky ground. No, I wasn't outside. I was in my own bedroom. My skates were gone, the hill was gone, and I was sitting on my rug.

I had fallen out of bed. My pillow was next to me and so was Tickly. I checked my plaster. It looked okay. Luckily, my arm didn't hurt.

"Karen!" Kristy burst into my room. She was wearing her nightie but she looked wide awake. That was when I realized that the long night was finally over. Sunshine was peeping through my curtains. My clock said 8:15.

Eight-fifteen! The last time I had looked at my clock it had said 6:59.

"What happened?" Kristy cried. She ran to me and sat down on the floor. I crawled into her lap. "How did you fall out of bed?" she asked. "Is your arm okay?"

It was scary falling out of bed with my plaster on, but my dream had been even scarier. "My arm is fine," I told Kristy. "But I didn't just fall, I fell off a cliff."

"You were dreaming."

"I know. It seemed real, though."

"Tell me about your dream."

So I told Kristy about the roller skates and the disappearing rabbit and the hill and the cliff. "There *was* no other side of the hill," I explained. "So I tried to turn around, but instead, I lost my balance and fell."

"Straight out of bed," Kristy added. "Poor Karen."

"Did I wake you up?" I asked. "I'm sorry if I did."

Kristy shook her head. "I was still in bed, but I was reading. Even if you *had* woken me up, I wouldn't have minded. Everyone has bad dreams sometimes."

Can you see why Kristy is one of my favourite people? Andrew and I are very lucky that she is our stepsister.

I got to my feet. I pulled open one of my curtains and sunshine streamed into the room.

"It's a gorgeous day," said Kristy. "It started off badly for you, but I'm sure things will get better now."

"Me, too," I replied.

"Why don't you get dressed? I'll help you."

(I can dress myself, of course, but it isn't easy with the plaster.)

"Okay," I said. "I think I'll wear my red shirt and my new jeans. The ones with the zips up the sides."

"The ones with the zips up the sides?"

repeated Kristy. "I don't think I've seen those before."

"No, you haven't," I said. "They're new. Mummy bought them yesterday."

"Where are they?" asked Kristy.

"In my bag," I replied.

Kristy looked through the things in my bag. "I can't find them," she said. She handed me the bag and I looked through it, too. No jeans.

"Oh no! I must have left them at Mummy's!" I wailed

"Never mind," said Kristy. "Listen, I have an idea. Put on your pink sweat-shirt and your normal jeans and your white trainers. Then I'll surprise you."

I grinned. A surprise? I love surprises! I let Kristy help me into my clothes.

"Now wait right here," said Kristy.

I waited. While I waited, I made my bed. (I had to do it one-handed.) Then I kissed Moosie good morning.

A few minutes later, Kristy came back. She was wearing jeans and white trainers and a pink sweat-shirt, too. "See? We're twins!" she cried.

"That's great!" I said.

But I still wanted my jeans with the zips. . . and wished that I hadn't fallen out of bed.

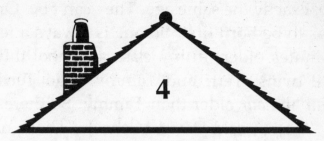

4

Those Nasty
Rice Crispies People!

Kristy and I went downstairs and into the kitchen.

Daddy, Elizabeth, Andrew, and David Michael were already there. They were eating breakfast.

"Well, well," said Daddy. "Look at our twins!"

I grinned. I felt very grown-up being Kristy's twin.

"They're not really twins," scoffed David Michael. "Real twins are exactly the same age."

17

"No they're not!" I said. "Real twins are *not* exactly the same age. They can't be. One has to be born first. So one is always a few minutes older. In my class at school there are twins, Terri and Tammy. And Terri's half an *hour* older than Tammy. So there."

"Gosh," said David Michael. "That's not what I meant. What I meant —"

"A-*hem*," interrupted Daddy. "That's enough. Kristy, Karen, are you hungry?"

"I am," said Kristy.

"I'm *starving*," I announced. "And I know what I want to eat — Rice Crispies."

"Too bad," said Andrew. "I've just finished the box — *and* I got the prize!"

My mouth dropped open. I looked helplessly at Daddy and Elizabeth. "You finished the box *and* you got the prize?" I said to Andrew.

He nodded.

"What was the prize?"

"Tattoos."

"Tattoos! That's the best prize of all!"

"We can share," said Andrew.

18

"Thanks," I replied glumly. I sat down at the table and put my chin in my hands. I had really wanted Rice Crispies.

"Karen," said Elizabeth.

"Yes?"

Elizabeth stood up. She went to the cupboard. "Look what I have," she said.

I looked. "Oh! a new packet of Rice Crispies. Thank you, Elizabeth! Thank you!" I jumped up. "Please can I look for the prize?" I asked her. *"Please*? Since Andrew got the other one."

"Well. . . I suppose so."

"Oh, goody! Thank you!"

Elizabeth got out a mixing bowl. She helped me pour the Rice Crispies into it. We poured and poured and poured — and at last the packet with the prize in slid out. I reached for it. I was about to open it when I realized something. Elizabeth had been awfully nice. I should help her put the cereal back in the box. So I held the box while Elizabeth carefully poured the cereal in it.

Then I poured a bowl of Rice Crispies for myself and added some milk.

I sat down at the table with my cereal and the packet.

I took one bite of cereal — and couldn't wait any longer. I opened the packet.

It was empty!

"It's empty!" I cried.

"Oh, no. Someone at the cereal company must have made a mistake," said Daddy.

I stared at the empty packet in dismay.

"Those nasty Rice Crispies people!" I said.

"Hey, Karen, you can still share my prize," said Andrew. "I'll give you half the tattoos, okay?"

"Okay. Thank you."

Andrew was going to share his prize with me, but I didn't have a prize of my own. And Kristy and I were twins, but I didn't have my jeans with zips. So far, the day was not very good. In fact, it was half bad. What would it be like if it were all bad? I wondered.

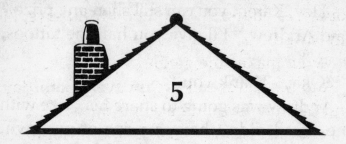

Goodbye, Mr Ed

When breakfast was over, I wandered into the study. I sat in a chair, pulled my knees up, and rested my chin on them. So far, Saturday didn't seem like a very good day. I looked at my watch. Nine twenty-five. It was still early! There was plenty of time for the bad day to turn into a good one.

Maybe a funny TV show is on *right now*, I thought. And that was when I remembered *Mr Ed*. *Mr Ed* is an old black-and-white show about a talking horse. A man sings a funny song like this: "A horse is a horse, of course, of course." And then Mr Ed says, "I am Mr Ed."

Mr Ed makes me giggle.

And *Mr Ed* repeats are on every Saturday and Sunday morning at nine-thirty.

I was just about to get up and turn on *Mr Ed* when Andrew ran into the study. He ran straight to the TV set, and turned it on. He switched it to Channel 5.

KA-POW! BLAM-BLAM-BLAM!

Andrew was watching cartoons.

I hate cartoons. At least, I hate the cartoons that Andrew likes. The only ones I like are Muppet Babies. Or cartoons with animals and fairies in them.

"Andrew," I said, *"Mr Ed* is on now."

Andrew had plopped himself on the floor right in front of the set. "So?" he replied.

"So I was going to watch it."

"Well, I'm watching cartoons."

"But I want to watch *Mr Ed*."

"But I want to watch cartoons."

"You can't."

"I already am."

I jumped out of my chair and I ran over to the television so I could change channels.

"Noooo!" howled Andrew, leaping to his feet. "Leave it alone. I got here first."

"Did not."

"Did too."

"Did not. Didn't you see me sitting right there?" I pointed to the chair.

"Yes. But the television was off."

"So what? I —"

"Hey, hey, *hey!*" exclaimed Daddy. He strode into the study. He was taking very big steps, which meant he was cross. Or at least not happy. "What's going on in here?"

"I wanted to watch *Mr Ed*," I told Daddy, "but Andrew turned on these stupid cartoons."

"Andrew, how long is your cartoon show?" asked Daddy.

Andrew shrugged. Daddy opened the *TV Guide*. "It's an hour long," he announced. "*Mr Ed* is only half an hour long. Karen, you may watch *Mr Ed*. After that Andrew, you may watch the rest of your programme. That way you'll each get to see half an hour of the show you like. Now, no more arguments."

Daddy left the room.

Wow! I thought. Great! Finally some good luck! I could watch *Mr Ed* after all. Even though I was glad about that, I stuck my tongue out at Andrew. I couldn't help it. He had made me angry.

I switched channels. I turned over just in time to hear an announcer say, "In order that we may bring you the following special programme, *Mr Ed* will not be seen this morning. It will return tomorrow at the normal time."

"Oh, no!" I cried. "*Mr Ed* isn't on."

Even the television people were giving me bad luck.

I looked at Andrew. Then I turned back to his show. "You can watch your cartoons, I suppose," I told him.

"Thanks," replied Andrew. "You can still have half the tattoos."

"Thanks."

I left the study. I looked at my watch. Nine thirty-one. There was still time for the bad day to turn into a good day.

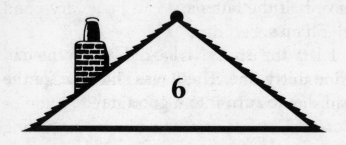

Boo-Boo's Boo-Boo

I wandered onto our back porch. I sat there with my chin in my hands, and looked out at our garden. The morning was cool and fresh. With the sun shining down, I didn't even need a jacket. My sweat-shirt would be warm enough.

I watched a squirrel chase another squirrel round and round and up a tree trunk, until they both disappeared in the branches. Then I watched two birds swoop low over the lawn. The animals seemed to be having fun.

Oh! Maybe that was what I needed — one of our pets. An animal can be a very good friend on a bad day.

I jumped up. I was ready to give the day another try. It was still only 9:45. I began to smile as I ran back inside to get Shannon or Boo-Boo. Maybe *now* would be the beginning of the good part of the day.

I found both Shannon and Boo-Boo in the living room. They were asleep on a sofa. It's funny — Boo-Boo is a cross old cat, but he's

always nice to Shannon. Even when Shannon is playing around, teasing Boo-Boo, Boo-Boo never hisses or swipes at her. And when they are both tired, they take naps together.

I think it's very nice of Boo-Boo to be so kind to Shannon. Just because Boo-Boo is nice to Shannon, though, doesn't mean he is nice to people. In fact, Boo-Boo is strange. He's always running and hiding, or scratching and biting.

If I wanted to play with a nice pet, it would be Shannon. But there are a couple of problems with that. For one thing, Shannon is really David Michael's dog. She doesn't know Andrew and me very well because she doesn't see us very often. For another thing, Shannon was asleep.

I lifted Shannon's ear. "Oh, Shannon," I whispered into it.

Shannon opened her eyes.

"Good," I said. "You're awake. Come on outside and play with me."

Shannon was a *very* sleepy puppy, but I

scooped her up and took her outside with me. She woke up straight away.

"Come on, Shannon! Chase me!" I cried.

Shannon chased after me. Then I threw a stick and she fetched it. I threw a ball and she fetched that, too.

Then I threw the stick again, but Shannon couldn't find it. She looked and looked.

"That's okay, Shannon," I called. "You don't have to find that stick. I'll throw you another one." But Shannon wouldn't stop snuffling around, looking for the stick.

Well, this was no fun.

Then David Michael came outside.

"Shannon!" he called.

Shannon ran to him. She forgot all about the stick *and* me.

I felt tears prick at my eyes, but I blinked them back. I'll just go and get Boo-Boo, I thought. So I did. It wasn't easy. Boo-Boo hissed at me because he didn't want to be picked up. But I hauled him outside anyway.

"Okay, let's play," I said to Boo-Boo.

Boo-Boo didn't look at me. He was staring at. . . Morbidda Destiny! She was in her herb garden next door.

"Hsss!" went Boo-Boo, and ran up a tree.

"Ha, ha, ha, ha, ha!" laughed David Michael.

But I didn't laugh. Nothing seemed funny to me.

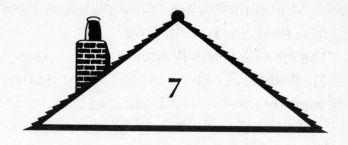

Fiddlesticks!

I ran to the tree that Boo-Boo had climbed.

"Boo-Boo!" I called. "Boo-Boo! Come down."

Boo-Boo wasn't listening. He had reached a high branch in the tree and was balancing on it.

I looked over at David Michael. He was throwing the ball for Shannon. They were having lots of fun. David Michael had forgotten about Boo-Boo and me and so had Shannon.

Well, I could have fun too. If I could just get Boo-Boo down, we could play and have a good time. . . couldn't we?

"Boo-Boo!" I called again. "Come down from there!" Then I added very softly, "Morbidda Destiny isn't going to hurt you." (I didn't want the witch to hear me.)

Boo-Boo didn't even look at me.

Ah-*ha!* I thought. Cat food! That always works. On television when a cat is up a tree, someone puts a dish of food on the ground, and the cat comes down to eat it. Simple!

I ran inside and poured Boo-Boo's favourite crunchy food into a saucer. Boo-Boo had just eaten breakfast, but so what. He hadn't eaten his crunchy food. He would want a treat.

I ran back outside and over to Boo-Boo's tree.

"Hey, Boo-Boo!" I called. "Look what I have for you!" I held up the dish of cat crunchies so Boo-Boo could see it.

He blinked his eyes. He stayed put.

34

I put the dish on the ground and waited. Nothing happened. Boo-Boo looked as if he might be getting ready to doze off. There was only one thing to do. I began to climb the tree. It wasn't easy, one-handed. But there were lots of branches to step on.

Boo-Boo woke up. He watched me climb towards him. He moved away from me.

Then, "Karen Brewer! You come down from that tree this instant!"

35

It was Daddy. He was shouting to me from the kitchen window.

I climbed down. I hadn't got very far anyway.

"Boo-Boo!" I called one more time. And then I gave up. I sat down next to the bowl of cat food.

Then Boo-Boo began edging down the tree. Great! I thought. But I didn't say anything. I knew that if I did, Boo-Boo would stay in the tree, just to make me angry. Instead, I watched Morbidda Destiny working in her garden. She looked very busy.

Suddenly, two things happened at once. Boo-Boo jumped to the ground. And in her garden, the witch exclaimed crossly, "Oh, fiddlesticks!" She began waving a rake around. Boo-Boo took one look at her and raced for the house.

Fiddlesticks. Was that a magic witch word? A spell for cats? Had Morbidda Destiny put a spell on Boo-Boo?

I didn't stay around to find out. I ran after Boo-Boo. If David Michael had any sense, he would come inside, too. And he would bring Shannon with him.

The witch was on the loose!

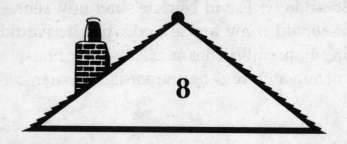

You're a Toad!

David Michael did run inside, and he brought Shannon with him. But I think he waited too long. I think Morbidda Destiny put a spell on him.

Why do I think this? Because David Michael was really nasty to me.

The first thing he said after he had closed the door behind him was, "Mu-um! I'm going over to Linny's."

"All right!" Elizabeth called back.

Linny Papadakis is David Michael's best friend. He and his family live over the road from us. Linny has two younger sisters. Sari is really little, but Hannie's my best friend. Well, she's my best friend when I'm at the big house. When I'm at the little house, I have a different best friend. (Her name is Nancy.)

Suddenly I felt like playing with Hannie. Maybe that would make my day better.

"I'm going with David Michael!" I called.

"No, you're not," he replied just as Elizabeth said, "Okay!"

"Yes, I am."

"No, you're not." (Can you see how nasty he was being?)

"Yes, I *am*. I want to see Hannie. I can go over there if I want to."

"Okay, but don't go with me."

"David Michael!"

Ding-dong.

David Michael and I both ran for the front door. We reached it at the same time. We had a fight over who would open it.

David Michael won. (I bet he wouldn't have won if he'd had *his* arm in plaster.)

Standing at the door were Hannie and Linny.

"Hi!" I said. "Guess what. We were just coming over to see *you*."

"You *were*?" said Hannie. "Good. That means you're free."

"Free?" I repeated.

"To go bike riding."

"Yes," said Linny. "We're riding to Harry's Brook. We're going to look for water spiders, and catch minnows and crayfish. We've even brought sandwiches for lunch."

"And biscuits!" added Hannie. "A real picnic."

"Great!" exclaimed David Michael. "Let me ask Mum if I can go."

David Michael ran off, but I just stood there. I glared at Hannie. Finally I said, "Well, thanks a lot."

"What's wrong?" asked Hannie.

"What's wrong?" I repeated. "What's *wrong*!" You know I can't go bike riding. That's what's wrong. I'm not allowed to ride my bike until my plaster comes off.

And I can't go wading in brooks, either. I
might get the plaster wet. How could you
be so mean, Hannie? You're a toad!" Hannie
was mean, too. Maybe *she* was under the
witch's spell.

"I am not!" yelled Hannie.

"Are so!"

"Am not so!"

"Are so too!"

"Am not so too!"

"Okay! I can go!" David Michael had come back. He was holding a bag of apples. "Mum gave us these for the picnic," he said. "Let's get our bikes."

David Michael and Linny left, but Hannie stayed behind. "You called me a toad," she said. "I'm *glad* you can't come with us. We wouldn't want you."

"Well, I wouldn't want to go on a picnic with a toad. So there!" I replied.

Hannie turned her back on me. I closed the front door. Why wasn't my bad day getting better? Was it all Morbidda Destiny's fault? Or was I just having an awful day?

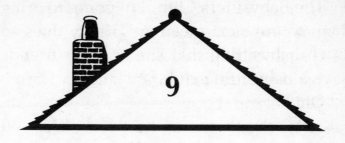

9

Winner, Loser

After I closed the door, I stood in our hallway for a few moments. The house was quiet. Elizabeth was in the study, sewing. Sam and Charlie were over at a friend's house; David Michael had gone on his stupid picnic; and Daddy had taken Andrew into town for a haircut.

Where was Kristy? Where was my twin?

"Kristy?" I called.

"I'm in the kitchen!" she replied.

I found Kristy putting a batch of cakes in the oven. "Hi, twin!" she said.

"Hi," I answered. "What are those for?"

"The Babysitters Club. I'm going to bring them to our next meeting." Kristy does so much babysitting that she and her friends have a babysitting club.

"Oh."

Kristy closed the oven door. "Do you want to play a game?" she asked.

I had a feeling Kristy was just being nice to me, but I did want to play with her, so I said, "We could play draughts." I'm good at draughts.

"Okay," replied my sister.

We found the draughts and set up the game in Kristy's room. She has a huge bed. It's so big that we could put the game in the middle and lie on our stomachs if we wanted to. That's a very comfortable way to play draughts.

"You go first," Kristy said.

I smiled. "Thanks!" That was nice of her. Kristy wasn't a toad.

The game began. I did a lot of jumping. Once, I got a triple jump. Jump, jump,

44

jump. Three of Kristy's pieces became mine. And *my* pieces were slowly crowned. They were made kings.

I gave Kristy a stern look. "Now don't *let* me win," I said to her. "I hate it when big people do that."

Kristy blushed. "Sorry, Karen. Okay. I'll play my best from now on. I promise."

The next thing I knew, Kristy got a triple jump. Jump, jump, jump. Then two of her pieces became kings. And the *next* thing I knew, Kristy had won the game.

"You beat me!" I exclaimed. I couldn't help looking a little cross.

"Well, you said not to let you win. So I didn't."

"But I'm good at draughts," I protested.

"Yes, you are," agreed Kristy.

"Then why didn't I win?"

Kristy sighed. She began to look more like a grown-up and less like my big sister. "Do you want to play again?" she asked. "Maybe you'll win this time."

"Okay," I said.

We set up the board for a second game. Then we started to play. Kristy played very badly.

But I got jumps and double jumps and triple jumps.

"King me! King me!" I said each time one of my pieces reached Kristy's side of the board.

After a while all of my pieces were kings

and none of Kristy's were. Also, I had jumped half of her pieces.

"You're not letting me win again, are you?" I asked.

"Well, I—I, um. . ."

"You are! You are letting me win!" I cried.

"But you were upset when I beat you."

"But I didn't want you to let me win!"

"Karen, I'm sorry. I'm really sorry," Kristy began.

I didn't hear what she said next, though. I had run out of her room.

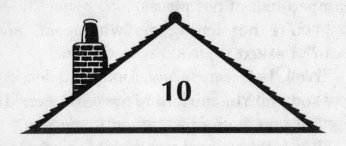

Moosie

I needed to hug something, so I went looking for Shannon. Now that David Michael had gone, maybe she would play with me. But Shannon was asleep. She was probably tired out from playing with David Michael. And Shannon is only good for hugging and playing when she's awake. So I left Shannon where I found her — curled up in the living room with Boo-Boo.

I went upstairs to my room. I would just have to hug Moosie and Tickly instead. I could play with them, too. They're not as much fun as Shannon and Boo-Boo are, but then, it was my bad day, so what did I expect?

I closed the door to my bedroom.

Then I ran across my room and leaped onto my bed. "Hello, Moosie-Moosie," I said. I gave Moosie a *very* tight squeeze.

Then I spread Tickly on the bed. I wrapped Moosie up in Tickly.

"Now you look just like a baby," I told Moosie.

I rocked Moosie in my arms for a while.

"Have you ever had a bad day? An awful day?" I asked Moosie.

Moosie looked at me with his round button eyes.

"Probably not," I answered myself. "A real cat might have a bad day, but not a stuffed one.

"Do you know what's happened so far today, Moosie? Everything. I had a bad dream, I fell out of bed, I forgot my jeans, the Rice Crispies prize packet was empty, *Mr Ed* wasn't on, Shannon wouldn't play with me, Boo-Boo ran up a tree, I had a fight with Hannie, and Kristy treated me like a baby. I think the witch is practising her spells."

I put Moosie back on the bed and unwrapped Tickly. "I think you need a new outfit, Moosie," I said.

I lifted up Moosie's T-shirt. Underneath I found a big rip. Moosie's stuffing was coming out!

I ran to my door and flung it open. "Elizabeth! Elizabeth!" I called.

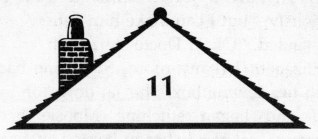

11

The Terrible, Horrible Day

Elizabeth came running. "Karen, what's the matter?" she cried.

I took Elizabeth by the hand and pulled her to my bed.

"Look at Moosie!" I exclaimed. "He's ill! He's dying! He's falling apart!"

Elizabeth picked up Moosie. She poked his stuffing back inside his tummy. She looked at the rip for a long time. Then she said, "I am the animal doctor, Karen. Do you give me permission to operate on Moosie?"

"I suppose so," I replied.

"He'll have a scar," Elizabeth went on seriously, "but I can make him better."

I smiled. "Okay, Doctor Elizabeth."

Elizabeth left my room. She came back with her sewing box. She sat down on my bed and began stitching Moosie back together. I sat next to her and rested my head against her shoulder. I watched the operation.

While Elizabeth worked, she said, "I think you've been having a bad day today, haven't you, Karen?"

"The worst," I agreed.

"Everybody has bad days," Elizabeth told me. "Do you know what happened on my worst day ever?"

"What?" I asked. Somehow, I hadn't thought of Elizabeth having bad days.

"Well, I was about sixteen."

"Older than Kristy?"

"Yes," Elizabeth answered. "And older than Sam. But not as old as Charlie."

I nodded.

"And all in one day," Elizabeth said, "I failed a test, my gym teacher yelled at me, I burned the chicken my family was having for dinner, I cut my hand, I had a fight with one of my sisters, and I lost my favourite ear-rings."

"That *is* pretty bad," I agreed.

"Do you know who else once had a bad day?" asked Elizabeth.

"Who?" I said.

"A little boy named Alexander. And there is a very funny book about his bad day. It's called *Alexander and the Terrible, Horrible, No Good, Very Bad Day*. Would you like to hear that story?"

"Yes," I answered. "And so would Moosie."

"Good," said Elizabeth, "because Moosie's operation is over and he's all well now. So why don't you wait here with him while I find the book? I think it's in David Michael's room."

"Okay," I replied. I held Moosie very gently until Elizabeth came back with the book.

We sat together on my bed and read it. It was funny and it was sad. Sometimes I laughed. Sometimes I said, "Alexander is just like me."

"How do you feel now?" Elizabeth asked me when the story was over.

"Much better," I said. "I think Alexander's day was even worse than mine. The dentist found a hole in Alexander's tooth. I've never had a hole."

"Do you know what? I have an idea of how you could turn your bad day into a good day."

"How?" I asked.

"Why don't you pretend the day is just beginning? You could start all over again. Here, lie down on your bed."

I lay down. Then Elizabeth said, "Karen! Karen! Time to wake up!"

I yawned and stretched.

"Is it morning?" I asked.

Elizabeth and I laughed.

"Yes," said Elizabeth. "Time to start a new day."

54

"Okay. I just know today is going to be wonderful!" I exclaimed.

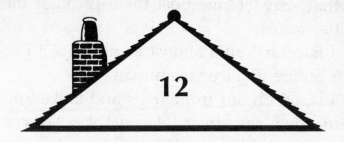

12

Here Comes
the Post Van!

I put Moosie on the bed. I covered him with Tickly. He needed to rest after his operation.

"Feel better," I whispered to Moosie as Elizabeth and I went downstairs.

"Guess what?" said Elizabeth. "It's almost time for the post. Why don't you run outside and see if Mr Venta is coming?"

"Okay," I said.

Mr Venta is our postman. He's very nice. Sometimes he lets me sit in his van and go down the street with him. He gives me the letters and lets me post them through the letter-boxes.

I like Mr Venta almost as much as I like Mr Softee, the ice-cream man.

I stood on our front steps and looked up and down the street. No post van. Maybe Hannie and Linny and David Michael would come home. I felt awful about yelling at Hannie. I wanted to tell her I was sorry. And I wanted to play with her.

But I couldn't see them, either.

I sat down on the steps. I watched a beetle in the grass. I read all the signatures on my plaster. Then I counted them. Then —

I heard squeaky brakes. I looked up. There was the post van!

Mr Venta was several houses away. Perfect. I could run to his van, climb on, and ride back to my house!

I took off. I'm not supposed to run fast with my plaster on, so I ran slowly. I jogged to the post van. It was at the Werners' house.

"Hi, Mr Ven —"

I stopped. Mr Venta was not driving the truck. A woman was driving it, and I had never seen her before.

"Do you live here?" asked the woman.

"No," I replied sadly. "I live down there." I pointed to our house.

Then I began walking home. I couldn't ask a stranger for a lift in the post van. That wouldn't be safe. Besides, I only like sitting with Mr Venta.

I could feel my bad luck coming back again.

It's a new day, it's a new day, I reminded myself as I waited by our front door. It isn't a bad day yet. Maybe something will come in the post for me! Maybe I'll get a letter. . . or a parcel! Even a sample would be good. I like samples of shampoo and hand lotion.

The post van crept towards me. At last it pulled up outside our house. I held out my hands and the lady gave me a pile of mail. On top of the pile was a parcel! I hoped it was for me, but I didn't look at the address.

I wouldn't look at it until I was sitting on our steps again. I would look at the rest of the mail first. Then I would look at the parcel. I would look at the return address, too. If I knew who it was from, maybe I could guess what it was.

"Thanks!" I called as the van pulled away.

I carried the post to our house. I was careful not to look at it. I sat down and I put the parcel under the letters. Then I looked at the letters. The first one was for Daddy. The second one was for Elizabeth. Then Elizabeth again, then Daddy, Daddy, Charlie, Elizabeth, Daddy, Elizabeth, David Michael, then two catalogues, and finally a magazine for Sam.

I was left with the parcel. I turned it over and read the address.

It was for Andrew.

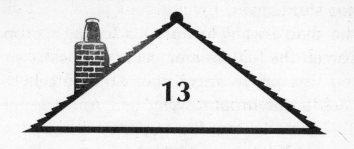

13

Mr Baldy

"Hello! We're home!" called Daddy.

Daddy and Andrew came into the kitchen. They were home from the barber. I was sitting at the table watching Elizabeth make hamburgers. Elizabeth had asked me what I wanted for dinner, and I had said, "Hamburgers, please."

The post was on the kitchen worktop.

"Hello," replied Elizabeth. "Andrew, you look very handsome."

I didn't say anything. I didn't think Andrew looked handsome. I thought he looked funny. The barber had cut his hair too short.

I didn't want to hurt his feelings, even though he *had* got a parcel in the post.

I was pretty angry about the parcel. In fact, I was furious. Why had Andrew got the prize in the Rice Crispies box *and* a parcel? If it was my bad day, it must have been Andrew's good day, maybe his best day.

The parcel was from Andrew's godparents. His godparents give him presents on his birthday and at Christmas and at lots of other times. Sometimes they send him a present for no reason at all.

I have godparents, too, and they do the same thing. But since today was my worst day and it was Andrew's best day, I didn't get a present and he did.

Maybe Andrew's present would be very, very boring. Maybe it would be socks or a sweater.

I pretended to be happy for Andrew, though. "Guess what," I said to him.

"You've got a present from Uncle Lou and Aunt Ann."

"I have?" cried Andrew. "Oh, great!"

I gave Andrew the parcel. He ripped the paper off. Inside a white box he found two videos — *Lady and the Tramp* and *The Secret of NIMH*.

Those weren't boring presents at all. They were wonderful presents!

I couldn't believe it.

"Wow!" cried Andrew. "New films! Look Karen!"

"Yes, I see."

"Let's go and watch them right now!"

"No way," I replied.

"Why not?" asked Andrew.

"Because I don't want to watch films with an egghead. You look like an egghead, Andrew. I think I'll call you Mr Baldy from now on."

Andrew's eyes slowly filled with tears.

"Karen," said Daddy sharply, "apologize right now."

"No," I replied. "Mr Baldy, you're so spoilt. And you won't like the films. That's the real reason I don't want to watch them. They are stupid and boring and awful."

"Are not!"

"Are too. You'll hate those rats of NIMH. You'll hate Nicodemus and Jenner. You'll hate Mrs Frisby, too. And Lady and Tramp and everybody in the other film."

"I will not!"

"Will too!"

"Karen," said Daddy in a very loud voice, "go to your room. Right now. I know you're having a bad day, but you may not take it out on Andrew. Please stay in your room for twenty minutes."

"O-*kay!*" I shouted.

I stormed up to my room as loudly as I could.

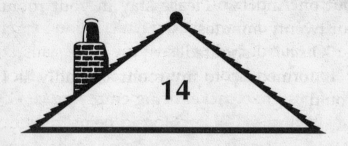

14

Karen's Punishment

It wasn't fair!

It wasn't fair that I got sent to my room for having a bad day.

After I had stamped up to my room, I grabbed my door and flung it — but I caught it just before it slammed. I shut it quietly. Daddy and Elizabeth don't like slamming doors.

I lay down on my bed with Moosie.

I cried for a while.

I had done everything I could think of to make my bad day better. Elizabeth had even helped me to start it again. I thought I had been very patient.

The bad day wasn't my fault. I didn't *mean* to fall out of bed or leave my new jeans at Mummy's. And I couldn't help the Rice Crispies prize packet being empty or *Mr Ed* not being on TV or Moosie being ripped. And I certainly couldn't help it that Aunt Ann and Uncle Lou had sent Andrew a terrific present on his best day. Anyway, it might all be Morbidda Destiny's fault.

And now *I* was being punished.

I wiped my eyes and blew my nose. "How are you feeling, Moosie?" I asked. I looked at his scar. It was neat and tidy. I could hardly see it. "I think you're feeling okay again, aren't you?"

I made Moosie nod his head.

After a while, I got up and went to my mirror. I stood in front of it. I made the saddest face I could think of. I stuck out my lower lip and pretended I was about to cry.

"Everyone hates me," I said, and felt even sadder. "Kristy hates me because I

acted like a baby. Daddy and Elizabeth and Andrew hate me because I was mean to Andrew. Hannie hates me because I yelled at her. Maybe Mr Venta even hates me. Maybe that's why he wasn't driving the van today."

Then I remembered a song. The worm song. "Nobody likes me," I sang sadly. "Everybody hates me. I think I'll go and eat worms. . ."

Er. That was a really horrid song.

I made an even sadder face and felt even sorrier for myself.

Then I flopped onto my bed. I picked up Moosie and pretended he was Andrew. "Karen, look at the new films I've got!" I made Moosie say in a high voice.

"You are so spoilt," I replied in my normal voice.

"Am not."

"Are too."

"Am not."

"Are too."

"Okay, I am spoilt. You're right."

"Let me have your films," I said.

"No."

"Yes."

"No."

"All right. Here they are. They're yours."

"Thanks. . . Mr Baldy."

That was how our fight should have gone. I sighed hugely.

I tiptoed to my door and opened it a crack. I listened. Nothing. I stuck my head into the hall. Nothing. I went out in the hall and peered between the banisters. Nothing. I couldn't see anyone or hear anything below.

So I went back in my room and just sat on my bed with Moosie in my lap. "Nobody likes me," I sang. "Everybody hates me. . ."

I sang the song ten times at the top of my voice before Daddy knocked on my door. He said my punishment was over. I had only been in my room for about fifteen minutes. I think he just wanted me to stop singing the worm song.

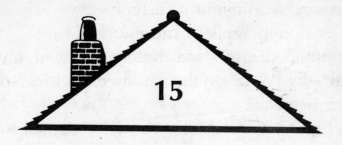

No More
Strawberry Ice-Cream

As I was leaving my room, I thought I heard a noise. It sounded like bells. I ran back into my room and looked out of the window.

Mr Softee was coming!

I grabbed some change that I keep in my jewellery box. Good luck at last! Mr Softee was coming just when my punishment was over, and I had enough money for an ice-cream.

I ran downstairs.

"Here comes Mr Softee!" I shouted to anyone who might be listening.

"Goody!" replied Andrew.

Both Andrew and Kristy followed me outside. We ran to the pavement and waved our hands.

Mr Softee was driving slowly up our street, bells clanging. Guess who was coming down the street in the other direction? Hannie, Linny and David Michael. Their picnic was over. They threw their bicycles down on our lawn and waited with Andrew and Kristy and me. A few moments later, Amanda and Max Delaney joined us. They live over the road from us. Amanda is my friend.

While we waited for Mr Softee. I glanced at Hannie. Was she still angry? Hannie looked at me and she smiled a tiny smile. I smiled a tiny smile back. Maybe things would be okay. At least we were smiling.

Ding-ding-ding-ding!

Mr Softee had arrived!

He stopped his van at the kerb and got out.

"Hello, kids," he said. "Hi, Karen. Hi, Hannie."

"Hello, Mr Softee!" we answered.

We all crowded around the van.

"Okay, okay! Form a queue," said Mr Softee. "That'll be much easier."

We formed a queue. Andrew was at the front. I was at the back. But I didn't care because I had money for ice-cream. In a few minutes, I would have a treat.

"Well, Andrew, what would you like?" asked Mr Softee. He adjusted his white hat.

"A Chocolate Feast, please."

"Right-o."

Mr Softee gave Andrew the Feast, and Andrew gave him some money.

Amanda Delaney was next, and she bought a Mint Feast.

What did I want? I leaned over to look at the ice-cream pictures on the van. I saw a lemon ice lolly and a Cornetto and a Double Choc and a Minimilk and. . . strawberry ice-cream!

A strawberry cone. That was exactly what I wanted.

The queue was growing shorter and shorter. Max and Linny and David Michael bought Cornettos. Hannie bought a Minimilk.

At last — my turn.

"I'll have a strawberry cone, please," I said to Mr Softee.

"Right-o." Mr Softee rummaged around in his van. He looked and looked. At last he said, "I'm sorry, Karen. I'm out of strawberry."

"No strawberry?!" I cried.

"No. But there's vanilla and chocolate and —"

"I wanted strawberry!"

"I'm very sorry, Karen."

I couldn't help it. I burst into tears and ran inside.

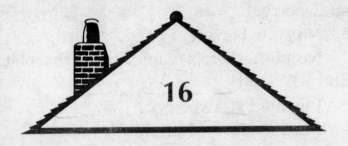

16

Karen's Worst Day

"Karen! Tea-time!"

Kristy was calling me. I was in my room rocking Moosie. I wasn't a bit hungry.

"I'm not hungry!" I yelled back.

A few moments later, Elizabeth called to me. "Karen, we'd like you to come and eat, please."

"But I'm not hungry," I replied. I hadn't even had a strawberry ice-cream and I still wasn't hungry.

"Please come anyway."

I stamped down the stairs. I dragged

myself into the dining room and slumped into my chair. I was the last person to sit down at the table.

Everybody was there: Daddy, Elizabeth, Charlie, Sam, Kristy, David Michael, and Andrew. They had already been served. A plate of food was at my place.

I stared at it. There was a hamburger and a baked potato and salad. I like all of those things. But I put my chin in my hands. I

didn't want to eat. My bad day had tired me out. I was too tired to eat.

"Well," said Daddy, after he had eaten a bite of his hamburger, "I suppose you had a bad day today, didn't you, Karen?"

I nodded.

"No Rice Crispies prize and no strawberry ice-cream," said Andrew sadly.

"No present and no *Mr Ed* and I fell out of bed and Moosie got ripped," I added.

"Last week," Sam said, "I had a bad day. I lost my homework and I stepped on Boo-Boo's tail. I felt awful."

"That's just two bad things, though," Kristy pointed out. "Once, my chair tipped over in English class and I'd forgotten my lunch money and my locker got stuck so I couldn't open it and I missed the bus home."

"Once I fainted in a school assembly," said Charlie.

We all laughed.

"But do you know what?" I said suddenly. "I've had the worst bad day of all. More bad things happened to me than to anyone else."

"I think you're right," agreed Kristy. "On my bad day, four things happened."

"Seven bad things happened to me on my worst day," said Daddy.

"How about you, Elizabeth?" I asked. "How many bad things happened on the day you told me about while you were operating on Moosie?"

"Let's see," said Elizabeth. She paused. "Six bad things."

"Okay," I replied. "Now let me count up my bad things." I used my fingers to help me. "I had a scary dream. I fell out of bed. I couldn't find my jeans. No Rice Crispies prize. No *Mr Ed*. Shannon wouldn't play with me. Then Boo-Boo wouldn't play, either. I had a fight with Hannie. I sort of had a fight with you, Kristy. Moosie got ripped. There was no Mr Venta. I didn't get any post. I got sent to my room for being mean to Andrew. And there was no strawberry ice-cream. Fourteen bad things. . . *Fourteen*!" (I left out the part about Morbidda Destiny's spell, because grown-ups don't like to hear about witchy things.)

"Gosh," said Kristy, "if there were a prize for bad days, you'd win it, Karen."

"I think," I said, "that this is the first good thing that's happened to me today. I set a bad-day record!"

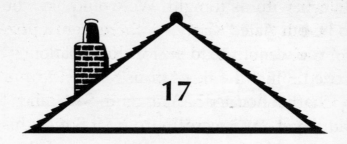

The Second Good Thing

As soon as I realized that I had set a bad-day record, I began to feel better. I even felt hungry. So I ate every bite of my dinner.

"Mmm," said Charlie as my family and I were cleaning up the kitchen later, "do you know what would taste good right now?"

"What?" I asked.

"Ice-cream."

"I don't think we have any."

"I know. That's why Sam and I were

wondering if you would come to Sullivan's Sweets with us tonight. We would like you to be our date."

"You want to go to the ice-cream parlour?!" I cried. "Just the three of us?"

Charlie nodded. "You and Sam and I didn't get any ice-cream from Mr Softee this afternoon. So we should take care of that. Will you come?"

"Yes please! If it's okay with Daddy and Elizabeth."

"It's okay," they said at the same time.

"Then let's go," said Sam.

I felt *so* grown-up. Charlie is old enough to drive, so we could go to Sullivan's Sweets all by ourselves. I sat in the back of the car and Sam sat in the front with Charlie. When we left our house, it was still light outside. I hoped somebody would see me. It wasn't every day I got to sit in a car and go to the ice-cream parlour with my big brothers.

Charlie drove us into town. He parked right in front of Sullivan's Sweets. We went inside and sat down at a small round table.

"So far, so good," I whispered to Sam and Charlie. "Nothing bad has happened."

Sam grinned. "Keep it up, kid."

Soon a waiter came to our table. "What'll it be?" he asked us.

Please, please, please don't be out of chocolate milkshakes, I thought.

"Karen?" asked Charlie. "Have you made up your mind?"

"I'll bet you don't have any chocolate milkshakes left, do you," I said.

"Of course we do. We can make anything," replied the waiter. "One chocolate milkshake coming right up."

"Goody!" I exclaimed.

Sam and Charlie each ordered a choc and nut sundae, and then the waiter left. When he came back, one chocolate milkshake and two choc and nut sundaes were on his tray.

"So far, so good," I said again.

Slurp, slurp, slurp. I sipped my milkshake. It was the best one I'd ever had.

We were just finishing our treats when

the door to Sullivan's opened. In came two big boys and two big girls.

"Hey!" exclaimed Charlie. "Hi, you lot!"

They all came over to our table. They were friends of Charlie's from high school.

Charlie introduced them. "This is John and Greg and Kate and Sandy," he said.

"And who's this?" asked John, pointing to me. "Do you have a new girlfriend, Charlie?"

84

I beamed. John thought I was old enough to be Charlie's girlfriend!

"No," replied Charlie, "this is my sister Karen."

"Do you have a boyfriend, Karen?" asked John. "Wait, don't tell me. You're married, is that right?"

I started to giggle. "No!" I cried. "People don't get married when they're six."

"You're only *six*? I thought you were *twenty*-six."

"No!" I said, still laughing.

Charlie and his friends talked about school for a while. Then his friends sat down at another table. It was time for us to leave.

"Goodbye!" I called as we left Sullivan's.

"Goodbye!" called John and Greg and Kate and Sandy.

"Thanks, Charlie. Thanks, Sam," I said. "Not a single thing went wrong at the ice-cream parlour. So that's the second good thing that's happened today."

We climbed into the car and drove home.

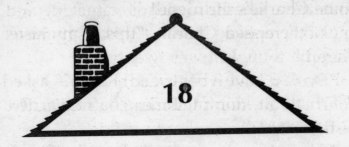

18

The Third Good Thing

Charlie pulled into our driveway. I jumped out of the car and ran inside. "Daddy! Elizabeth! Kristy!" I exclaimed. "Guess what!"

The rest of my family was watching TV in the study. But when they saw me, they turned off the television.

"What is it, darling?" asked Elizabeth.

"Everything went right! Charlie found a parking place in front of Sullivan's. And they had chocolate milkshakes. I wanted a chocolate milkshake more than anything.

Even more than a strawberry ice-cream. And then Charlie's friends came in, and one of them asked if I was Charlie's *girlfriend*! Then he thought I was twenty-six!"

Elizabeth and Daddy laughed.

"That's wonderful, darling," said Daddy. "And now, guess what time it is."

"Time to get ready for bed?" I asked.

"Exactly. Time for Andrew and David Michael, too."

My brothers' eyes met mine. We grinned at each other. "Let's go!" I said.

We ran up the stairs. We have a bedtime secret. No one knows about it but us. It's the special way we brush our teeth.

The three of us gathered in the bathroom. We loaded our brushes with toothpaste. Then we brushed and brushed and brushed until our mouths were just full of foam. I had to brush left-handed because of my cast.

When we could not keep the foam in our mouths any longer, I said, "Okay, one, two, three, spit," only it sounded like, "Unh, two, fee, pit."

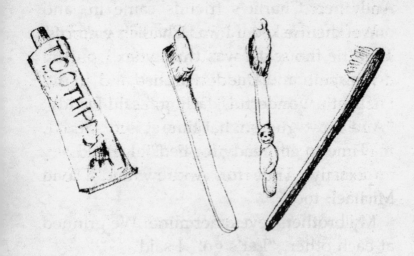

We spat.

I had never seen so much toothpaste foam in the sink. Neither had David Michael nor Andrew.

"We did it!" I said. "We set another foam record."

"I'll say," agreed David Michael.

"And I was brushing left-handed. So this is a very special record."

"*Very* special," echoed Andrew.

"Guess what. This is the third good thing

that's happened. I suppose my bad day is really over."

We left the bathroom. I was in a terrific mood. I felt so happy, that, after I put on my nightie, I went downstairs and found Elizabeth. I had to ask her something.

"Elizabeth," I said, "before I go to bed, may I do three things? They're really important. And they won't take a long time."

"All right," agreed Elizabeth.

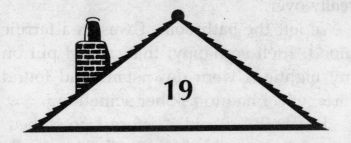

19

I'm Sorry

My three important things were apologies. I needed to say "I'm sorry" to Andrew and to Hannie and to Kristy. I started with Andrew, since he had to go to bed soon.

"Andrew?" I said. I stood at the door to his room. He was sitting on the floor, looking at a picture book.

"Yes?" said Andrew.

"Can I come in?"

Andrew nodded.

Then he and I sat on his bed. I drew in a

deep breath. "Andrew," I said, "I'm really really really sorry I called you an egghead and Mr Baldy. That wasn't nice at all. But I was feeling rotten because of my bad day."

"That's okay," said Andrew.

"Do you know something? Today Elizabeth read me a story. It was about a boy who has an awful day. It's called *Alexander and the Terrible, Horrible, No Good, Very Bad Day*. It's David Michael's book. Do you want me to read it to you? If I read it, you might understand how I felt. And why I yelled at you."

"Okay," said Andrew.

I borrowed the book from David Michael. Then I read it to my little brother. "You see?" I said. "The worse the day is, the crosser you feel."

Andrew nodded. "I see. . . Karen?"

"Yes?"

"You can still have half my tattoos. And you can watch my new films whenever you want."

"Thanks, Andrew."

I left Andrew's room. It was time for my next apology. I went into the kitchen. I phoned Hannie.

"Hi, Hannie," I said. "It's me, Karen."

Hannie didn't say anything.

"I know you're angry," I went on. "I'm sorry I called you a toad. But do you know what? Today was my worst day ever. It was so bad, I set a bad-day record. Fourteen bad things happened."

"*Fourteen?*" cried Hannie.

"Yup." I listed them for her. Then I told her about the good things. Well, not about the foam record, since that's a secret. But I told her the other things.

"A big boy asked if you were Charlie's girlfriend?" squeaked Hannie. "That's really great."

"I know," I said. "Then he thought I was twenty-six!"

"Karen!" called Elizabeth. "Time for bed."

"I have to go, Hannie," I told her, "but I'll see you tomorrow, okay? We can play dolls. And I won't call you a toad."

"Okay," said Hannie, and we hung up.

Elizabeth was standing in the doorway to the kitchen. "Do you want Kristy to put you to bed?" she asked.

Kristy usually puts me to bed.

"Yes," I answered. "I'll say goodnight to you and Daddy now."

"Okay." Elizabeth took my hand. We walked into the study.

I crawled into Daddy's lap and kissed his nose. "Goodnight," I said.

"Goodnight," said Daddy.

Then I gave him a butterfly kiss with my eyelashes.

"Elizabeth?" I said as I got out of Daddy's lap. "Can I tell you something?"

"Of course." Elizabeth sat down.

I put my hands around one of her ears and whispered, "Thank you."

Elizabeth put *her* hands around one of *my* ears. "For what?" she whispered back.

I giggled. "For mending Moosie and reading the story about Alexander to me."

"You're welcome," Elizabeth replied.

Then we gave each other butterfly kisses and I went upstairs.

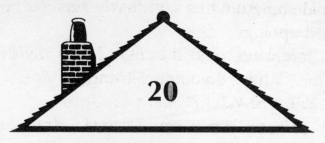

20

Goodnight, Karen
Goodnight, Kristy

"Karen! Karen!" Kristy was calling me from upstairs.

"Coming!" I answered.

I ran up the stairs. Kristy had just put Andrew to bed. He goes to bed first since he's the youngest. After I go to bed, it's David Michael's turn.

Kristy was waiting in my room. I climbed into bed and hugged Moosie.

"Well," said Kristy, "what story shall we read? *The Witch Next Door*?"

The Witch Next Door is my favourite story.

I did want to hear it. But not straight away. I had something to say. It was time for my third apology.

"Before we read a book," I told my big sister, "I have something to say to you."

"You do? What?"

"I'm sorry. I'm sorry about the draughts game. I wasn't nice to you."

"I *was* letting you win, though," said Kristy, "and that wasn't nice of me, either."

"But you were *trying* to be nice," I pointed out. "I was just feeling too awful to notice. So I'm sorry."

"In that case," said Kristy, "I accept your apology. I promise I'll never let you win again, though. The next time you win, it will be because you played a good game."

"Maybe the next time I win will be on a good day!" I exclaimed. "If today was my worst day, then some time I'll have a best day. That will probably be a draughts-winning day."

"I hope so," said Kristy. "Now how about a story?"

96

"Okay, but you choose. Any book you want." (I know Kristy gets tired of reading *The Witch Next Door*.)

"Really?" said Kristy. "How about if we begin a new book? I could start reading *Charlotte's Web* to you. You'd really like it."

"Okay," I agreed, "Have I got that book?"

"No, but I have. I'll go and get it. I'll be right back."

While Kristy was in her room, I talked to Moosie. "You're going to hear a new story," I told him. "Try to listen quietly. No interrupting."

Kristy came back with the book. "Did anything bad happen while I was gone?" she teased me.

"Oh, Kristy," I said.

Kristy read the first chapter of *Charlotte's Web*. Then she told me about the rest of the book. The story was going to be about a girl named Fern Arable, who lives on a farm, and her pet pig Wilbur and a clever spider called Charlotte A. Cavatica. Kristy was right. I would like the book.

When Kirsty finished the first chapter, she closed *Charlotte's Web*.

"Do you think pigs ever have bad days?" I asked her.

"Wilbur does. You'll see."

"What about witches?" I asked. "Do you think they ever have bad days?"

"Oh, yes," replied my sister. "They mix up their potions all wrong and their spells go wrong and their broomsticks won't fly.

Kristy and I laughed.

Then I snuggled under the duvet. Kristy kissed me goodnight. Then she kissed Moosie. She turned on my night-light. As she was leaving the room she said, "I'm *sure* tomorrow will be a good day."

What a relief. I couldn't think of anything nicer.

"If that's true," I explained to Kristy, "then that is the fourth good thing about my bad day."

"Goodnight, Karen."

"Goodnight, Kristy."

JUGGLERS

There are books to suit everyone in Hippo's JUGGLERS series:

Pet Minders	Robina Beckles Willson	£1.75
The Jiggery Pokery Cup	Angela Bull	£1.75
The Ghosts of Batwing Castle	Terry Deary	£1.75
Stan's Galactic Bug	John Emlyn Edwards	£1.75
My Friend Robinson	Anne Forsyth	£1.75
As If By Magic	Jo Furminger	£1.75
Bags Of Trouble	Michael Harrison	£1.75
The Spooks	Elizabeth Lindsay	£1.75
The Secret Of Bone Island	Sam McBratney	£1.75
School Trip To The Stars		£1.75
Horrible Henry and The Headless Ghost		
	Kara May	£1.75
When I Lived Down Cuckoo Lane	Jean Wills	£1.75

You'll find these and many more fun Hippo books at your local bookseller, or you can order them direct. Just send off to Customer Services, Hippo Books, Westfield Road, Southam, Leamington Spa, Warwickshire CV33 0JH, not forgetting to enclose a cheque or postal order for the price of the book(s) plus 30p per book for postage and packing.

THE BABYSITTERS CLUB

Need a babysitter? Then call the Babysitters Club. Kristy Thomas and her friends are all experienced sitters. They can tackle any job from rampaging toddlers to a pandemonium of pets. To find out all about them, read on!

The Babysitters Club No 1:
Kristy's Great Idea £1.75
The Babysitters Club No 2:
Claudia and the Phantom Phone Calls £1.75
The Babysitters Club No 3:
The Truth About Stacey £1.75
The Babysitters Club No 4:
Mary Anne Saves The Day £1.75
The Babysitters Club No 5:
Dawn and the Impossible Three £1.75
The Babysitters Club No 6:
Kristy's Big Day £1.75
The Babysitters Club No 7:
Claudia and Mean Janine £1.75
The Babysitters Club No 8:
Boy Crazy Stacey £1.75
The Babysitters Club No 9:
The Ghost at Dawn's House £1.75
The Babysitters Club No 10:
Logan Likes Mary Anne! £1.75
The Babysitters Club No 11:
Kristy and the Snobs £1.75
The Babysitters Club No 12:
Claudia and the New Girl £1.75
The Babysitters Club No 13:
Goodbye, Stacey, Goodbye £1.75
The Babysitters Club No 14:
Hello, Mallory £1.75

GREEN WATCH by Anthony Masters

GREEN WATCH is a new series of fast moving environmental thrillers, in which a group of young people battle against the odds to save the natural world from ruthless exploitation. All titles are printed on recycled paper.

BATTLE FOR THE BADGERS
Tim's been sent to stay with his weird Uncle Seb and his two kids, Flower and Brian, who run Green Watch – an environmental pressure group. At first Tim thinks they're a bunch of cranks – but soon he finds himself battling to save badgers from extermination . . .

SAD SONG OF THE WHALE
Tim leaps at the chance to join Green Watch on an anti-whaling expedition. But soon, he and the other members of Green Watch, find themselves shipwrecked and fighting for their lives . . .

DOLPHIN'S REVENGE
The members of Green Watch are convinced that Sam Jefferson is mistreating his dolphins – but how can they prove it? Not only that, but they must save Loner, a wild dolphin, from captivity . . .

MONSTERS ON THE BEACH

The Green Watch team is called to investigate a suspected radiation leak. Teddy McCormack claims to have seen mutated crabs and sea-plants, but there's no proof, and Green Watch don't know whether he's crazy or there's been a cover-up . . .

GORILLA MOUNTAIN

Tim, Brian and Flower fly to Africa to meet the Bests, who are protecting gorillas from poachers. But they are ambushed and Alison Best is kidnapped. It is up to them to rescue her *and* save the gorillas . . .

SPIRIT OF THE CONDOR

Green Watch has gone to California on a surfing holiday – but not for long! Someone is trying to kill the Californian Condor, the bird cherished by an Indian tribe – the Daiku – without which the tribe will die. Green Watch must struggle to save both the Condor and the Daiku . . .